Watercolour Ponies
Copyright © 1992 by WORD Publishing

Managing Editor: Laura Minchew
Project Editor: Brenda Ward

Library of Congress Cataloging-in-Publication Data
Watson, Wayne, 1954-
Watercolour ponies / by Wayne Watson; illustrated by Sandra Shields.
p. cm.
"WordKids!"
Summary: Just as her mother grew up and left her parents to start a family of her own, April grew up and has her own child to continue the cycle of life.
ISBN 0-8499-0976-7
[1. Parent and child—Fiction.] I. Shields, Sandra, 1956- ill. II. Title.
[E]—dc20   PZ7.W3318Wat   1992

Printed in the United States of America
2 3 4 5 6 7 8 9 R R D 9 8 7 6 5 4 3 2

WATERCOLOUR PONIES

WAYNE WATSON

Illustrated by Sandra Shields

WORD
kids!

WORD PUBLISHING
Dallas · London · Vancouver · Melbourne

To my wife, Lynn,—always faithful and generous with her sweetness, bestowed on everyone she meets and permanently implanted into the hearts of my sons, Neal and Adam. Any tenderness in their hearts is there by the grace of God and the love of their mom.

There are watercolour ponies

On my refrigerator door,

And the shape of something I don't really recognize;

Brushed with careful little fingers

And put proudly on display,

A reminder to us all of how time flies.

"What a beautiful baby," said Grandma Martha.
Little April looked up at her with big blue eyes.
"How time flies! It seems like only yesterday
that your mommy was this little."

Martha remembered all the fun times
when her daughter Catherine was little:
the new puppy...swinging in the park...
going to Mr. Robert's farm to ride the ponies.

Now Martha was a grandmother.
And as she held her new grandbaby for the
first time, she said:
I love you more than I can say,
More than words can tell.
And though I hold you close today,
You'll someday, one day ride away.

Grandma Martha brought some wonderful gifts
for little April: a stuffed bunny, a soft pink blanket,
and one very special gift
that was most precious to her.
"I've been saving this for you, April."

It was a simple painting of a pony.
Little April couldn't know just
how special the picture would be...
at least not right now.

Even April's daddy and mommy didn't
pay much attention to the watercolour pony at
first. Catherine hadn't remembered painting it
for her mother so many years ago.

When April took her first step,
Mommy and Daddy beamed with pride.
Daddy held April in his arms and said:
I love you more than I can say,
More than words can tell.
And though I hold you close today,
You'll someday, one day ride away.

Late one night, little April was crying.
Her favorite pink blanket was wet
with tears, and her fever was very high.
Though April was becoming such a big girl,
she still needed her mommy and daddy.
Some nights, as they rocked her to sleep,
they would whisper Grandma's words.

Catherine smiled and smiled as she helped
April dress for her first day of school.
"Bye, Mommy," April called out.
"I love you sweetie," Catherine said,
loud enough for April to hear.
"More than I can say," she said quietly
to herself.

"You're quite a young lady, April."
"Oh, Daddy, please let me go to the party.
All my friends will be there!"
All your friends, thought her father,
are not my little girl.

"Is everything packed, honey?"

"I think so, Mom."

"Wow, I'm really going off to college," she sighed.

"Mom, is it okay to be a little afraid?"

"You or me, dear?" asked Catherine.

April packed her clothes and all her favorite things.
She glanced at the simple painting of a pony
that her grandmother had given her so long ago.
She'd never understood why it was so special to everyone.
Once again, she read the words on the back of the frame.

April's baby boy was
born on the first day
of spring.

There were new flowers
in the yard and a nest
of baby birds singing.

She and her husband
had hoped and prayed
for this day.

April couldn't believe she was a mommy.
With her son in her arms, she
remembered when she was a little girl.
Time had passed so quickly.

Grandmommy Catherine and Grandaddy Joe
flew on an airplane to visit their new grandson.
Grandaddy Joe held a brand-new baseball glove
in his lap. "The perfect gift for my fine grandson,
don't you think?" he said.

Grandmommy had a special gift, too.

The beautiful box she held was all wrapped in silver with a fine blue ribbon. There was a small card attached to the outside, and it read:

Boys to men do quickly pass,
Childhood days go by so fast.
Hold this dear one while you may.
He'll someday, one day ride away.

April opened the box her mother gave her. Inside was the simple little painting of a pony in a brand-new blue frame.

"It's for the baby's room," Grandmommy said smiling. "I've been saving this for you, little fellow."

There on the back of the picture
were the same words April had read all her life.
She had never really understood them before,
but now, the meaning was very, very, clear.

I love you more than I can say,
More than words can tell.
And though I hold you close today,
You'll someday, one day ride away.

There are watercolour ponies
On my refrigerator door,
And the shape of something I don't really recognize;
Brushed with careful little fingers
And put proudly on display,
A reminder to us all of how time flies.

Seems an endless mound of laundry
And a stairway laced with toys,
Gives a blow by blow reminder of the war
That we fight for their well being,
For their greater understandin'
To impart a holy reverence for the Lord.

But baby, what will we do
When it comes back to me and you?
They look a little less like little boys ev'ry day.
Oh, the pleasure of watchin' the children growin'
Is mixed with a bitter cup
Of knowin' the watercolour ponies
will one day ride away.

And the vision can get so narrow
As you view through your tiny world,
And little victories can go by with no applause.
But in the greater evaluation,
as they fly from your nest of love,
May they mount up with wings as eagles for His cause.

Still, I wonder baby, what will we do
When it comes back to me and you?
They look a little less like little boys ev'ry day.
Oh, the pleasure of watchin' the children growin'
is mixed with a bitter cup
Of knowin' the watercolour ponies will
one day,—one day ride away.